PUFFIN BOOKS

SUPERPOWERS

THE RAGING BULLS

Books by Alex Cliff
SUPERPOWERS series

SUPER
THE RAGING BULLS
POWERS

ALEX CLIFF

ILLUSTRATED BY LEO HARTAS

PUFFIN

PUFFIN BOOKS

Published by the Penguin Group

Penguin Books Ltd, 80 Strand, London WC2R ORL, England

Penguin Group (USA) Inc., 375 Hudson Street, New York, New York 10014, USA

Penguin Group (Canada), 90 Eglinton Avenue East, Suite 700, Toronto, Ontario, Canada M4P 2Y3
(a division of Pearson Penguin Canada Inc.)

Penguin Ireland, 25 St Stephen's Green, Dublin 2, Ireland (a division of Penguin Books Ltd)

Penguin Group (Australia), 250 Camberwell Road, Camberwell, Victoria 3124, Australia
(a division of Pearson Australia Group Pty Ltd)

Penguin Books India Pvt Ltd, 11 Community Centre, Panchsheel Park,
New Delhi – 110 017, India

Penguin Group (NZ), 67 Apollo Drive, Rosedale, North Shore 0632, New Zealand
(a division of Pearson New Zealand Ltd)

Penguin Books (South Africa) (Pty) Ltd, 24 Sturdee Avenue, Rosebank,
Johannesburg 2196, South Africa

Penguin Books Ltd, Registered Offices: 80 Strand, London WC2R ORL, England

puffinbooks.com

Published 2007

2

Text copyright © Alex Cliff, 2007
Illustrations copyright © Leo Hartas, 2007
All rights reserved

Set in Bembo
Typeset by Palimpsest Book Production Limited, Grangemouth, Stirlingshire
Made and printed in England by Clays Ltd, St Ives plc

British Library Cataloguing in Publication Data
A CIP catalogue record for this book is available from the British Library

ISBN: 978-0-141-32139-4

www.greenpenguin.co.uk

For Peter, for everything, but most of all for
hearing the clipper-clapper and for always
knowing what I wish to sing.
(Stephen Crane: There was a Man
with Tongue of Wood*)*

CONTENTS

Just imagine . . .   1

One   Who Will it Be?   5

Two   Despair!   17

Three   The Raging Bulls   30

Four   Bucking Bronco!   40

Five   Taming a Bull   53

Six   The Battle Begins!   64

Seven   The Symbol in the Wall   76

Eight   The Power of Fellowship   88

Nine   Scars   99

JUST IMAGINE . . .

the grey stone walls of a ruined castle on a hillside. Beyond the castle walls, a dark moat glitters. It is quiet and peaceful, apart from the occasional caw of a group of ravens perched on the castle walls.

CRASH!

A thunderclap echoes around the castle keep. The ravens fly into the air in alarm as a hawk with cruel eyes swoops out of the blue sky. The hawk lands beside the castle's one remaining tower. As it lands, it changes into a very tall woman. A cloak of brown-grey feathers swirls from her shoulders and her black eyes flash angrily. This is the evil goddess Juno.

She snaps her fingers and the stones on the inside of the tower wall start to crumble away. A man's proud face appears. He grabs the edges of the hole. 'Today is the day, Juno!' he roars. 'Today I will get the last of my superpowers back!'

'Never, Hercules!' Juno cries. 'I will not stand by and watch it happen!'

Hercules thumps his fist into the wall of the tower. 'Seven tasks, you have set those two boys. They have succeeded in six. If they complete the final task today, I will get the last of my superpowers back and will be able to break free from these walls. Then –' he glares at her – 'then you will be sorry!'

'But you will *not* get the power back today!' Juno shrieks. 'The boys must bring twenty raging bulls back to the castle. No mortal could ever do that. The bulls will trample and gore them. They

will not survive. And when they die so do your chances of escape, Hercules. If you do not escape today your final superpower will fade and be lost to you forever!'

'The boys will not fail me!' Hercules exclaims.

They stare at each other. Then Juno swings round angrily and snaps her fingers. The stones close over Hercules' face.

'I will win!' Juno hisses, staring out at the castle keep. 'I will!'

CHAPTER ONE

WHO WILL IT BE?

'Your call,' Max said nervously. He and Finlay were sitting in his bedroom. Max looked at the coin in his hand. 'Here goes.'

'Heads!' Finlay called as Max flicked up the coin.

Finlay and Max both held their breath as they watched it spinning in the air.

A week ago, their lives had changed

forever. They had discovered the ancient
hero, Hercules, trapped inside the walls
of the ruined castle outside their village.
Juno had taken his superpowers during
a fight between Hercules and her and

placed them in the stones of the castle's
gatehouse. Finlay and Max had been
determined to free Hercules, and so
each day, for seven days, they faced a
terrifying task set by the evil goddess.
These tasks would have been impossible
for a normal human to complete but
each day either Max or Finlay got to
choose one of Hercules' superhuman
powers to help them. Juno had made a
deal with them that if they completed
the task by sunset the superpower
returned to Hercules. Today was the
day of the final task.

The coin spun down.

Max caught it and covered it with his
hand.

'Well?' Finlay demanded.

Max slowly revealed the coin.

A mixture of relief and disappointment crossed his face. 'It's heads.'

Finlay let out a deep breath. 'Looks like I get the superpower of incredible-agility, then. I'll be able to run, climb and jump like a superhero.'

Max forced himself to smile. 'And you'll have the chance to herd twenty raging bulls.'

'Let me at 'em!' Finlay said with a shaky grin. 'You'll help, though, won't you?'

'You know I will,' Max replied, looking determined. 'We're going to do this task and get Hercules his last superpower back!'

'Then he can break free from the tower and fight Juno!' Finlay jumped to his feet and leapt forward, doing a karate chop.

'Hi-yaa!' He tripped over a pile of Max's books. 'Oof!' he exclaimed as he landed on the floor.

'Hope Hercules does better than that if he fights Juno!' Max grinned.

Finlay picked himself up. 'Ow,' he said, inspecting a recent cut on his leg. Blood was seeping out of it. 'I'll be glad when all our wounds heal over.'

Every day either Max or Finlay had been injured while carrying out Juno's tasks. It was always the person with the superpower who seemed to get injured and each wound looked suspiciously like the symbols of the superpower they had taken that day. Max looked at his own three wounds – one on his hand, one on his leg and one on his arm. 'I hope they turn into proper scars. That would be cool!'

'I just hope I don't get another one today!' Finlay said. 'What do you reckon these bulls will be like?'

'I dunno but I looked up some stuff on the Internet last night,' Max replied eagerly. He loved finding things out. 'There was loads about bulls.'

'But did it tell you what wild magic bulls conjured by psycho goddesses are like?' Finlay said.

Max grinned. 'No, but I found out some general facts that might be useful.' He tried to remember what he'd read. 'You can lead a bull around by putting a ring through its nose. If they're together in a group there's always one big boss bull that all the other bulls will follow. They hate red. Oh, and their horns are very sharp – they can kill a man by goring him.'

Finlay groaned. 'Oh, great, and we've got twenty of them to try and herd.'

'Least we don't have to kill them,' Max said, looking on the bright side.

'Yeah, we've just got to stop them from killing us!' Finlay took a deep breath and went to the door. 'Come on, let's go. I need to get that superpower!'

Each morning, just as the sun shone on the gatehouse wall, the bricks crumbled from around Hercules' face, so he could see out of the tower and the superpowers lit up in the stones of the gatehouse. They shone for twenty minutes and the boys had to take the superpower then.

'Where are you two off to?' Max's mum asked as Max and Finlay went into the kitchen.

'The castle,' Max replied.

'You'll be moving in there next!' Mrs Hayward smiled. 'Are you still looking for the dungeon?'

'Oh . . . um, yes!' Max said. On the

first day of half-term, six days ago, he
and Finlay had set off to try and find
the castle's secret dungeon, but then of
course they had met Hercules and their
plans had changed. Still, his mum didn't
know that. No one did!

'Oh well, I suppose you'll be there
all day again,' Mrs Hayward said. 'You'd
better take some lunch with you. I'll just
get it ready.'

It seemed to take Mrs Hayward forever
to make the lunch. 'That's enough, Mum,'
Max said anxiously, as his mum started
to butter even more bread for about the
seventh round of sandwiches. He looked
at the kitchen clock. Time was ticking by.

'I'll just do you a few more,' his mum
said cheerfully. 'Can you find the picnic
basket and rug, please, Max?'

'Picnic basket!' Max stared at her. 'Can't we just have a carrier bag, Mum?'

'Everything will get squashed,' his mum said, looking at the mound of sandwiches and chocolate cake. 'You might as well use the basket. You can tie it on to the back of your bike.'

Max exchanged looks with Finlay. He was going to feel really stupid cycling up to the castle with a picnic basket on the back of his bike but he didn't want to waste any more time by getting into an argument with his mum. 'OK,' he muttered.

He fetched the basket and the red checked rug. His mum packed everything inside with four cans of Coke and some apples. 'Have a good day, then!'

'Thanks, Mum!' Max grabbed the basket and he and Finlay ran outside.

'I thought we were going to be trapped in your kitchen forever!' Finlay exclaimed.

'I can't believe we've got to take a picnic basket with us!' Max said.

'At least the food looks good!' Finlay

replied, thinking of the chocolate cake he'd seen Mrs Hayward cutting up.

They hastily strapped the picnic basket on to Max's bike.

'Come on!' Max exclaimed to Finlay. 'Let's go!'

CHAPTER TWO

DESPAIR!

The cycle ride to the castle was all uphill.
The boys stood on their pedals and
cycled as fast as they could.

'At least we'll be able to use our bikes
to cycle to wherever these bulls are,'
Finlay said as they bounced over the grass
and stones on the overgrown footpath.

'I hope Juno tells us where they are,'
Max replied. Juno had a sneaky habit of

17

leaving them to search for the monsters
they had to fight.

The castle came into view. The boys
rode up to it and jumped off their bikes.
Leaning them against the crumbling
walls, Max and Finlay climbed through
the ruined gatehouse and came out
into the grassy castle keep. The sun
was shining on the gatehouse wall and
Hercules was already looking anxiously
out of the tower.

'Get the superpower quickly, boys,
before Juno arrives,' he called urgently.
'She will want to do everything she can
to try and stop you succeeding in the
task today!'

Max and Finlay saw the last of the
seven symbols shining out of the stones
around the gatehouse archway. It was a

picture of a stag leaping through the air
– the symbol for Hercules' superpower
of agility. Finlay raced over to it. The
picture was traced in lines of white magic

fire. He slammed his hand down on it. Heat surged through his fingers and up his arm. He felt dizzy. Every muscle in his body suddenly seemed to buzz with energy. The stone beneath his fingers went cold.

Finlay turned round. 'I've got it!'

He ran across the grass, back towards the tower. He didn't go much faster than normal but he felt light and full of energy, as if he could dodge and duck and turn without any effort at all. 'Look at me!' he shouted, jumping high into the air and turning a somersault. He landed perfectly. 'Cool, hey?' He grinned at Max and Hercules.

CRASH!

There was a clap of thunder and Juno appeared in the middle of the keep. Her dark eyes flashed. Finlay hastily raced over to join Max.

'Today is the day you fail!' she hissed, raising her hands. The boys instinctively shrank back. When Juno lifted her hands a fire bolt usually burst from them.

'You must not hurt the boys, Juno!' Hercules shouted. 'You have a deal with them. They can be injured by the task but you cannot harm them directly. You know the rules – you must play fair when you deal with humans!'

'Maggots!' spat Juno, firing a ball of fire so it landed at Finlay's feet. He gasped and leapt to the side, dragging Max with him, just in time before the flames touched them.

'Juno!' Hercules roared furiously. 'You are breaking the rules!'

Juno glared at Max and Finlay but to
their relief stopped throwing fireballs. 'I
might not be supposed to kill you while
we have a deal, but you will be injured
by the task today – fatally injured!' Her

voice rose and echoed around the castle
walls. 'You will not survive the twenty
raging bulls of Geryon! They are twice
as strong as normal bulls, and their horns
are twice as sharp!'

'We don't care!' Finlay declared.

But Max could hear the shake in
Finlay's voice. His own legs felt like
jelly but he ignored the way they were
trembling. 'Yeah! We'll bring those bulls
back! Where are they?' he demanded.

'Find out for yourselves!' Juno's eyes
pierced the boys like a spear through a
fish.

'Boys,' Hercules shouted quickly, 'you
will need to . . .'

'No!' Juno shrieked. 'No advice today!'
She clapped her hands. There was a crash
of thunder; the wall re-formed over

Hercules' face. The boys blinked. Juno
had vanished.

A hawk raced up into the sky, its dark
eyes glittering savagely.

'She's mad!' Finlay said, very relieved
that Juno had gone.

Max nodded. His heart was pounding.
'I hope we can bring these bulls back
here.'

Finlay gulped. 'Me too.'

For a moment they saw the doubt in
the other one's eyes.

'Max, we *are* going to be able to do
this, aren't we?' Finlay said.

Max lifted his chin. 'Yes.' He tried to
make his voice sound firm. They couldn't
let Juno win. They mustn't let Hercules
down. 'Think of all the tasks we've
done this week. Everything's seemed

impossible but we've managed to do them all.'

'You're right,' replied Finlay. 'We've come this far. We're *not* going to fail now.' He took a deep breath. 'Let's go find us those bulls!'

'Where should we look?' Max asked eagerly.

Finlay remembered the time they'd been looking for the Nine-Headed River Monster, only to find that it had been in the castle moat all the time. 'We should probably try the countryside near here first.' He looked at Hercules' tower and had an idea. 'I know! I'll use my superpower and climb to the top of that tower to have a look round.'

'Good idea,' agreed Max.

Finlay ran to the tower wall and

leapt up on to it, his hands and feet automatically finding stones that could be used as handholds and footholds. He climbed swiftly up the tower, one hand above the other. It was cool! He felt like Spider-Man.

Reaching the top, Finlay gripped the stones of the ledge and jumped lightly into a crouching position. He looked down at the keep and waved to Max, who was looking very alarmed.

'Be careful, Fin!'

Finlay grinned. He was way up high, but he felt totally safe. His balance was perfect. He glanced round at the green fields and woods that surrounded the castle. From his vantage point, he could see the wooded slopes of Saddleback Mountain, where they had chased the

savage Giant Boar of Erymanthia.
Dotted between the trees was a patchwork
blanket of fields. There were some golden
cows grazing quietly in one field, a few
horses in another, an empty field and . . .

Finlay's heart seemed to stop.

Twenty enormous black bulls were charging around the next field along. Their horns were curved and very long. The ones who weren't charging were pawing savagely at the ground and bellowing angrily. As he watched, the largest bull of all raced at the fence. The bull's horns crashed into the wood. It shook with the impact. The bull shook his head and prepared to charge again.

Icy fear gripped Finlay. If the fence gave way then the bulls would be free. The path their field was on led down into the village. If the bulls got out on to it they would stampede into the village centre . . . How many people would they injure or kill?

'Can you see anything?' Max shouted.

'Yeah!' Finlay shouted back. He swung

himself over the ledge and began to climb down the tower as quickly as he could. 'The bulls are in one of the fields by the woods, Max! Come on! They're going to break the fence down! We've got to be as quick as we can!'

CHAPTER THREE

THE RAGING BULLS

'So what did the bulls look like?' Max gasped as they jumped on their bikes.

'Big.' Finlay thought of the bull that was attacking the fence with its pointed horns and red eyes. 'And very, *very* scary!' He began to cycle down the hill. 'They're in one of the fields over this way,' he said, turning on to a track between two fields. 'One of the bulls was destroying the fence. If he breaks out, all the bulls will be free!'

'How are we going to stop them?' Max said. 'We haven't got anything to use. No weapons. Nothing. Fin! One bull would be bad enough. How are we ever going to deal with twenty?'

But for once even Finlay was out of ideas. 'I don't know,' he panted. 'We'll think of something though. We have to!'

Reaching the end of the path they heard the sound of fierce bellows and the stamping of hooves. They swung on to another farm track and then both skidded to a halt. At the end of the track was a field. It was full of twenty enormous black bulls.

'Oh, pants,' Max breathed, staring at the bulls.

Finlay felt his stomach somersault. The
bulls had been terrifying enough when
he'd seen them from the top of the tower,
but to see them this close was a million
times worse. They were huge! Their long

horns ended in deadly sharp points. The
muscles under their black coats rippled.
Their red eyes glittered as they stamped
the ground and tossed their heads. The
biggest bull gave a loud bellow and
charged at the fence again.

'Argh!' the two boys yelled as they
leapt back in alarm. The bull's tank-like
chest crashed into the wooden planks.

The horizontal slats gave a loud creak
as the wood cracked slightly, but it held
firm. The bull shook its head and walked
back, preparing to charge again.

'It's going to break if he charges again!'
Max said in alarm.

Finlay made a decision. He had
the superpower. It was up to him to
do something. Maybe if he caused a
distraction . . . He raced towards the

fence, waving his arms. The big bull
stared at him with its vicious red eyes.
'Come and get me, then!' Finlay yelled
at it.

'No!' Max gasped as Finlay grabbed
the top of the fence and vaulted over. He
landed lightly in the field. Two bulls, one
on either side of him, lowered their heads
and charged straight at him.

The ground shook with the thunder
of their hooves. *Run!* Finlay's mind
screamed at him as the bulls bore down
on him. But he didn't. He held his
ground. They got closer and closer. His
heart felt as if it was about to leap out of
his chest.

Now! he thought. And at the very
last second, just as the bulls' horns were
sweeping down through the air towards

him, Finlay put one foot on to the fence
behind him and sprang straight up into
the air, somersaulting into the field and
out of their reach. There was no way the
bulls could stop in time. They crashed
into each other, bellowing furiously as
their horns got tangled up.

OK, now *run!* Finlay thought.

He began to race through the herd,
weaving and ducking and jumping like a
character in a computer game.

As two other bulls galloped towards
him, Finlay dodged out of the way,
and grabbed the horns of a third bull.
He swung himself up on to its broad
black back. The bull snorted angrily
and bucked. But Finlay had already
leapt agilely through the air and landed
perfectly on the back of the next bull

along. The bull whose back he had stood
on first, charged the second in its attempt
to attack Finlay, but he simply leapt to
the back of the next bull along and left
the two furious beasts to it.

He sprang from back to back. The
bulls went berserk. They didn't seem very
clever and they charged wildly at each
other in their attempts to get to him.
Soon the field was echoing with bellows
of pain and fury.

'Fin! Get out of there!' Max felt sick.
If Finlay slipped and fell, then the bulls
would gore or trample him. To his horror,
he saw the biggest bull – the one who
had been attacking the fence – fix its
vicious eyes on Finlay. A bellow burst
out of it and it charged. The other bulls
scattered. None of them seemed to want
to get in this bull's way.

It must be the leading bull, Max realized,
remembering what he'd read about bulls
the night before on the Internet.

'Fin! Watch out!' he shouted as the

leader bull lowered its head and galloped faster.

Seeing it approaching, Finlay leapt once more and this time grabbed an overhanging branch of a nearby tree. His hands caught the branch firmly and he swung himself up.

The enormous leader bull stopped by the tree and glared up at him. Pawing the ground with its hoof and snorting, its mean eyes glowed red.

'Can't get me, you great big brainless beef burger!' Finlay taunted it.

The branch he was sitting on suddenly made an alarming creaking noise.

Max gasped. A large crack splintered through the branch. It started to bend. It was going to break.

'No!' Max shouted as, with a creaking, cracking noise, the branch snapped away from the tree.

With a yell of alarm, Finlay began to fall . . .

CHAPTER FOUR

BUCKING BRONCO!

Finlay felt the superpower tingle through him as he fell through the air. He flung himself forward on to the grass in a smooth roll and jumped effortlessly to his feet. The only problem was that he found himself standing just a few metres away from the bull! He stared straight into its mean red eyes. It lowered its head to charge again.

Finlay instantly sprinted away, dodging
and ducking through the other bulls.
They scattered. Suddenly there was
nothing ahead of him except an empty
green field; and nothing behind him

except a crazed bull seconds away from
spearing him on its horns. *What can I do?*
Finlay thought. The answer flashed into
his mind. *Surprise it!*

He threw himself straight at the
ground, twisting to one side on his
shoulder as he hit the grass and rolled out
of the way.

The bull couldn't stop in time to turn
and get him, but it swept its horns round
as it careered past. Finlay yelled in pain
as the bull's left horn caught his side,
ripping his T-shirt and leaving a jagged
cut. He rolled on the ground, clutching
the wound.

The bull came to a stop and lumbered
round heavily to face him again. Finlay's
blood dribbled down its horn on to its
furious face.

'Move, Fin!' Max yelled. But Finlay was still holding his side in shock.

I've got to do something, Max thought desperately. He looked round. His eyes fell on the red picnic blanket attached to his bike. Bulls hated red things. He raced over, grabbed the blanket, and scrambled over the fence. 'Hey, bull! Look at this!' he yelled, trying to distract it by waving the rug.

The bull's eyes flickered to him then back to Finlay, who was slowly standing up.

'Yeah, over here!' Max shouted, waving the rug at his side like a bullfighter. 'Look at this lovely red blanket! Come and get it!'

With a snort, the bull charged straight at the blanket. Max had never been more

terrified in his entire life. He whisked
the blanket up into the air and the bull
charged past.

'What are you doing? You're not a
bullfighter! Get out of here, Max!' yelled
Finlay. He started to run, wincing at the
pain in his side.

'Not till you do!' Max retorted.

The bull had turned. It pawed the
ground. 'It must be the leading bull
of the herd,' Max said quickly. 'Look
how the others are staying away from it.
If we can control it and make it come
with us, then maybe the others will
follow.'

'Control it! It doesn't exactly look
controllable to me, Max!' exclaimed
Finlay as the bull galloped towards them
again.

Max threw the blanket up away from him but he was a fraction too late. This time the bull caught the material on its horns. It tossed the blanket into the air and as it landed on the ground the bull ripped it into shreds. Roaring a bellow of rage, it galloped straight at the boys.

'Move it, Max!' Finlay yelled. 'Get out of the field!' He ran out into the middle of the field to try and distract the bull but it charged past him – and with a sick feeling Fin realized it had fixed on to Max as an easier target.

Run! Max thought, suddenly remembering that he didn't have a superpower or even the blanket now. Sprinting for the fence, he glanced over his shoulder; the charging bull was bearing down on him. Its horns were going to get him. He pushed himself even harder, even faster, until he couldn't tell the pounding of his heart from his footfalls as he tore over the springy turf . . .

Suddenly the thunder of the bull's hooves stopped. Max looked round over his shoulder in surprise. What had happened?

'Fin!' he gasped, skidding to a halt.

Finlay had seen the bull charging past him towards Max, and at the last moment had sprung into the air, landing perfectly on the bull's back! The bull was now only interested in getting him off. Ignoring the pain in his side, Finlay threw himself forward so that he was sitting just behind the bull's neck on its mighty shoulders.

Chucking its head down, the bull began to kick its back legs up like a bucking bronco in a rodeo. Finlay threw one arm back, and hung on to the bull's neck with his other hand. His knees gripped the bull's shoulders. 'Wahey!' he

yelled, his eyes alight with a mixture of
fear and excitement as the bull plunged
around the field, its head down, its
hooves kicking upwards, its great muscles
bunching and heaving.

Max gazed, open-mouthed. Finlay
might be super-agile but he couldn't
hang on forever. Max looked back at
the fence and an idea came to him. He
picked up the torn blanket then ran
forward, waving it at the bull. Catching
the flash of red, the bull stopped for a
second and looked up.

'Come on! This way!' Max yelled.

'What are you doing?' Finlay shouted
as Max started running towards the fence
with the bit of blanket.

Max didn't reply. The idea was still just
forming in his head. He looked at the

fence ahead of him. He reckoned that
with its head lowered the bull's horns
were about the same height as the top
slat of the fence. If he could just get it
to charge into the fence with its horns
lowered then maybe . . .

There wasn't time to think any more.
The bull was galloping after him with
Finlay clinging to its back. Hoping
desperately that his plan would work,
Max raced up to the fence.

He chucked the blanket through the
gap between the first and the second
slats and dived after it, head first. As he
crashed on to the ground on the other
side of the fence, he heard Finlay yell in
shock and then the fence shook as the
bull's nose and muzzle shot between
the slats. Its horns pierced into the top

slat, the force of its heavy body driving
the pointed tips straight through the
sturdy wood and out the other side.
Finlay was thrown over the bull's head.
He fell, tumbling through the air like an

acrobat, and landed, with a gasp, on both feet without even so much as a wobble. He offered Max his hand, who took it gratefully and scrambled up.

They turned to survey the leading bull. Its muzzle was shoved between the slats and its horns were trapped in the wood of the top slat. It tried backing up but its horns wouldn't come free. It bellowed in frustration and stamped a hoof, however there was nothing it could do. It glared at Max and Finlay. It was caught fast.

'We've caught it!' Finlay exclaimed. 'It's stuck! That was a cool idea, Max.'

Max's heart was still pounding. 'I didn't know if it would work or not. I thought the bull might crash straight through the fence!'

'But it didn't!' Finlay grinned. 'Now

that's what I call taking a bull by its horns!'

Max looked at the trapped bull and then at the field where the other bulls were milling around. 'We might have trapped it, but, Fin, how are we going to get it and the other bulls back to the castle?'

CHAPTER FIVE

TAMING A BULL

Finlay looked at the bulls. Max had a
point. How could they possibly get all
twenty bulls back?

Max looked at the bull that was stuck
in the fence and frowned. 'I wish it had a
ring through its nose. We could use that
to lead it and then maybe the
others would follow. It is the lead bull,
after all.'

Finlay peered at the bull. 'It has got holes where a ring should be.'

'Bet Juno took its ring out to make things harder for us,' Max groaned.

'Hang on, we might not have a ring,' Finlay said thoughtfully, 'but we could use something else. We just need something that will go through those holes. Maybe we could use some string or rope or . . . yes, I know!' He ran over to the picnic basket and pulled off the cord that attached it to Max's bike. 'This will do! We can put this through the holes in its nose and make a ring from it!'

'Brilliant idea!' Max exclaimed.

Finlay went up to the bull. It tried to shake its head but the fence held firm. The other bulls were watching. They

didn't look mad any more, just anxious;
now they could see their leader was in
trouble their furious bellows had faded to
wary snorts and low rumbling moos.

Finlay reached forward gingerly. 'Urgh!

Its nose is all snotty!' he said, looking at the bull's foam-flecked muzzle and nose. 'I'm going to get bull's bogies on me!'

'Here, I'll do it!' Max liked animals and didn't mind anything to do with them. He took the strap from Finlay and went up to the bull. Trying not to look too closely at the bull's strange glaring red eyes, he carefully pushed the end of the cord through one of the holes in the bull's nose and out through the other side. He tied the ends in a firm knot so that it formed a ring between the bull's nostrils. As he took hold of the ring, the bull sighed and some of the fire in its eyes seemed to die.

'You know, I think this might work,' Finlay said. 'It doesn't look nearly so mad now. I bet we'll be able to lead it.'

'First, though, we've got to get its horns out from this fence,' Max pointed out. He examined the way the bull's horns were jammed through the wood. He had no idea how they could get them out. 'It looks almost impossible. We'll need a saw or something.'

'Or my screwdriver!' Finlay pulled his penknife out from his pocket. The knife bit was small and useless but it had lots of clever gadgets on, including a screwdriver. 'If we can't take the bull's horns out of the wood, we'll just take the wood with us instead!' Finlay began to unscrew the plank of wood from the fence posts. 'I'll take it off the fence and the bull can just carry it!'

Max shook his head in wonder. 'Sometimes you have really cool ideas!'

'Well, I can't help being naturally brainy,' Finlay said airily as he unscrewed the other side of the plank. 'Just call me a genius.'

The bull snorted. Slobber and foam flew out of its mouth and nose, covering Finlay's torn T-shirt.

'Yuk!' Finlay yelled, pulling a face.

Max grinned. 'You're a snot-covered genius now!'

The bull lifted its head. The plank of wood was still attached to its horns but it was free. Keeping a careful hold on the cord through the bull's nose, Max climbed over the rest of the fence and led the bull through the other bulls towards the gate. 'Come along, boy.'

Finlay rolled his eyes. 'He's not a dog, Max!'

'Now he's stopped trying to kill us, I actually kind of like him.' Max went to pat the bull's nose but the bull tossed its head angrily away. The plank of wood swung round. Max ducked just in time. Finlay grabbed him and stopped him from falling over.

'OK, less of the Dr Doolittle stuff, Max,' he said grimly as the bull glared at them with its red eyes. 'Let's just get this lump of beef stew with bogies back to the castle.'

He ran on ahead and opened the gate. The other bulls jostled to one side to let Max and the lead bull past. Finlay watched them. Would they follow?

He needn't have worried. As soon as the lead bull was through the gate, the other bulls walked out tamely too.

'I think this is going to work!' Finlay
shouted in excitement.

Max was holding on to the cord
through the bull's nose and watching

warily for any sudden movements. A
thought struck him. 'If we get them all
back to the castle, we'll have completed
the task!'

'And then Hercules will be free!' Finlay
exclaimed. 'Let's go!'

They made a strange procession as they
walked up the hill, with Max leading the
main bull and the other nineteen bulls
following. Finlay raced around behind
them, making sure all the other bulls kept
up. They had to leave their bikes and the
picnic basket behind.

'We'll come back for them later,' Max
said. 'I just hope we don't meet anyone
on the way back to the castle.'

Luckily they didn't.

'We're almost there!' Finlay exclaimed

as the castle came into view. They led
the bulls up the hill and on to the bridge
that crossed the castle moat. As the leader
bull crossed the bridge and reached the
gatehouse there was a bright flash of
lightning and suddenly all twenty bulls
vanished!

'We've done it!' Finlay exclaimed.
'We've completed the last task!'

'Come on!' said Max.

The boys scrambled through the
gatehouse. As they emerged into the
keep, Finlay felt a warm swirling in his
chest. The next second golden light
flooded out of him and streamed across
the keep towards the tower. It was the
superpower returning to Hercules! As
it flooded through the tower wall the
stones in the wall began to fall.

'Look, Fin!' Max gasped as the stones smashed to the ground faster and faster.

With a crash, Hercules burst free from the tower!

CHAPTER SIX

THE BATTLE BEGINS!

Hercules stood inside the tower surrounded by fallen stones. As the dust cloud cleared he stepped forward over the rubble. His long hair fell down to his shoulders, his face looked young again – the deep wrinkles had gone – and his golden eyes glowed like a lion's. One hand held a sword and the other a shield.

'You have released me!' he exclaimed, his strong voice ringing out across the keep. He strode out of the tower over the stones, a delighted smile on his face. 'You have restored all seven of my superpowers! You are *true* heroes!'

But as he strode across the keep towards them, a fork of lightning cut jaggedly down through the sky and there was a thunderclap so loud that the walls of the castle seemed to shake.

Juno appeared. Her face was twisted with rage. In one hand she was holding a ball of white fire that blazed so brightly neither of the boys could look at it. 'No!' she shrieked. 'You shall not escape from me, Hercules!'

She swept the burning ball up into the air.

Within a second, Hercules had his shield up. 'Get back, boys!' he yelled. Max and Finlay raced to take cover in the gatehouse. The fire bolt hit the shield and exploded in a shower of white burning arrows that shot through the air.

The boys watched as Hercules leapt towards the goddess, his sword at the ready. She clicked her fingers.

'She's going to freeze him!' Max exclaimed. But Hercules was ready. In the same instant as Juno's fingers snapped a magic barrier formed around him.

'That may have worked on the boys, but I know all your tricks, Juno,' he shouted, and as he did so he stooped to lift a heavy boulder in each hand. He catapulted the first boulder straight at Juno's head. And then before the first boulder had even reached her he had let the second boulder fly straight at her middle.

Juno did not even blink. With a deft flick of each arm, she turned her feather cloak into two wings, one raised in front of her head, the other just below. She flexed her arms and the wings seemed to glow with a sharp metallic light. As the boulders hit each wing they bounced harmlessly, one to each side, leaving Juno with an exultant smile.

'Ah yes, Hercules,' she gloated, letting her feather cloak fall back to her side. 'You know my tricks. But I know *your* tricks even better. There isn't one of your powers that can harm me.'

'We'll see about that!' Hercules ran to the tower wall. Without even slowing down he sprang effortlessly up it. A moment later a massive stone roof slab was hurtling down from the tower straight at the goddess.

The boys gasped. Hercules himself was balancing on the slab as if it were a surfboard, using all his superpowers to keep it on course.

Finlay grabbed Max's arm. 'He's going to land on her!'

The goddess tensed. A second before the slab was about to hit her she clicked the fingers of each hand. Where she

had been standing there was suddenly
nothing but a flurry of brown feathers.
Hercules yelled in alarm. He'd obviously
expected the slab to hit Juno and not
the ground. The slab smashed down and
dust and shards of stone flew in every
direction.

The boys stared at each other in shock
– surely no one, not even a superhero,
could survive that collision. And yet,
moments later Hercules was rising
groggily out of the dust cloud. But he
got no further than to his knees before
a whirlwind of feathers began and Juno
reappeared. Without any hesitation
she took one step towards the winded
Hercules and kicked him savagely back
to the ground. As she did so she
clapped her fingers again and with a

sickening crack Hercules' body snapped helplessly flat on to the broken slab of rock.

'We have fought this battle before. I will send you back into the tower wall,' Juno cried. 'You are powerless now. One bolt of magic and you will be imprisoned forever!' She raised her hands, a smile playing around her mouth as she savoured the moment of having Hercules at her mercy. 'And this time there will be no deals and *no* escape!'

'Max! We've got to do something!' Finlay said desperately.

'I know! But we haven't got any superpowers or weapons!' Max exclaimed.

Finlay saw Juno's hands clench. They might not have any weapons or

superpowers but they couldn't stand by
and watch as she sent Hercules back into
the wall again – not after everything they
had been through to free him. Finlay
looked round. There must be something
they could use. Suddenly he saw a nearby

flat rock. He grabbed it and raced out
across the keep.

At exactly the same time, Max
charged out, too, thinking that maybe if
he could distract Juno then it would give
Hercules a chance to recover. 'Over here,
Juno!' he shouted, just as he had done
with the bull when Finlay had
been injured.

The goddess started in surprise just as a
lightning bolt shot out from her hand.

'No!' yelled Finlay, leaping in front
of Hercules, holding the rock up like a
shield. It exploded into pieces, the force
of the blast sending Finlay rolling over
and over on the ground.

'Brave but foolish boy!' Hercules
gasped weakly.

Juno swung back round furiously. 'How

dare you interfere!' she hissed to Finlay. 'Pathetic human!'

Finlay lay on the ground. The fall had knocked all the air out of his lungs. He felt like a ten-ton truck had just driven over his chest.

Juno stalked over to him. Her eyes glittered. 'I have not been able to kill you before now because I had made a deal with you. But the deal is now over.'

'Yes, cos we won!' Finlay gasped painfully.

Juno smiled. 'And now it is I who shall win! You chose to get involved in this battle between me and Hercules, miserable human. Now accept the consequences. Alone, without superpowers, you have no chance against me!'

Finlay staggered to his feet just as Max raced to his side. 'But he isn't alone!' Max yelled fiercely. 'We're in this together!'

'Then you will die together!' Juno exclaimed. She raised her hands, her eyes savage and triumphant.

Side by side, Max and Finlay braced themselves, and waited for the final blast . . .

CHAPTER SEVEN

THE SYMBOL IN THE WALL

Juno sent a ball of white lightning hurtling towards Max and Finlay's heads.

'No!' Hercules roared as the boys screwed their eyes shut.

Finlay tensed, expecting his body to be blown into a million tiny pieces. But nothing happened. A strong force, like a whirlwind, seemed to be tearing round him, pulling at his hair and clothes, but there was no pain. He opened his eyes. He and Max were surrounded from their head to their toes by a swirling dome of white light.

'Max!' he gasped. 'Look!'

Just as Max opened his eyes, the dome broke up and the light streamed past

them. It hit the gatehouse wall behind them. There was a loud bang and a crack spread out from the base of the wall across the ground.

Max and Finlay both jumped out of the way as the crack rapidly spread towards them. Max frowned. There seemed to be an underground chamber or something beneath the crack.

But before he could say anything or look further, Hercules was staggering to his feet, relief sweeping over his noble face. 'Time and again you have broken the rules of the gods in your dealings with these boys this week, Juno, and now this is the price you pay!' he roared. 'The gods have seen fit to protect them against your evil.' He swung round. 'Run!' he urged Max and Finlay. 'The gods have

looked after you this once to act as a
lesson to Juno but I do not know if they
will protect you again. Go! I will deal
with her!'

'Never!' Juno screamed furiously. She
shot a ball of fire at him but Hercules was
ready with his shield. The bolt exploded,
sending arrows of deadly fire flying
around the keep. Max grabbed Finlay's
arm. 'Quick!' he exclaimed. 'We've got to
take cover!'

Jumping over the crack in the ground
and the underground chamber, they
raced towards the gatehouse. As they
did so, Finlay saw something shining
on the wall. 'What's that?' he exclaimed,
pointing.

Max followed his gaze. Around the
archway, just where Juno's lightning bolt

had hit, a new symbol was suddenly glowing. 'I don't know,' he said. He ran closer and saw that it was a picture of two hands clutched around a sword.

'Do you think it's another superpower?' Finlay said.

'It can't be,' Max replied. 'Hercules only had seven.'

'So what is it, then?' demanded Finlay.

'Maybe it's something to do with the gods,' Max answered. 'You know, that stuff Hercules was saying about the gods protecting us.'

Finlay nodded. 'It came when the light hit the wall. I know! Let's touch it and see what happens!'

'Hang on,' Max said quickly. 'What if it's not the gods? What if it's a trick of Juno's?' He frowned. 'What if it *kills* whichever of us takes it?' They glanced round. Hercules was now wrestling with Juno, pinning her arms to her sides. She clicked her fingers and the next instant she had turned into a hawk and was streaking upwards out of his arms and away. With a savage cry, she circled in the sky in her hawk-like form and then swooped straight at Hercules' face, talons and beak outstretched. He ducked but her claws raked down his cheek. As she landed, she turned back into a woman in the blink of an eye and flung another bolt of fire at him. He staggered backwards with an alarmed cry.

'We haven't got many choices, Max,' Finlay said quickly. 'We can run away . . .'

'*Never!*' Max said fiercely.

'Well, then, we can wait here till Juno defeats Hercules and then see what she does to us . . .'

Max didn't say anything.

'Or we can try taking this superpower and see what happens. Which should we do?'

Their eyes met. It was obvious. There was no decision to be made.

'We take the superpower!' Max exclaimed.

Finlay nodded. 'Which one of us? I guess it *is* your turn, Max . . .'

Max heard the disappointment in Finlay's voice. He looked at the two hands clasped around the sword and a thought struck him. Why should just one of them take the power? Before, when

they had the deal with Juno, that was
what they'd agreed with her, but this
wasn't part of that deal. 'Let's both take
it! If you want to of course,' he added
quickly.

'Of course I want to!' Finlay
exclaimed. He looked at Max. 'Let's do
it now!'

Hearts racing, they stepped forward
and banged their hands down on the
stone together. Heat flooded into them,
just like when they had taken the other
superpowers. Max felt it surge through
his fingers, down his arms and all the way
through his body to his toes.

The stone turned cold underneath
their fingers.

He and Finlay looked at each other
uncertainly.

'I feel all tingly, as if I've got a superpower,' Finlay said slowly. 'But what do you think the power is?'

'Guess there's only one way to find out,' Max said. 'We try doing stuff. Hey, look at me!'

He jumped on a large boulder and

then began to climb up the gatehouse wall. His hands naturally seemed to find bricks to take hold of and he climbed quickly and easily all the way to the roof. 'I can climb!' he said. He jumped down, turning a perfect somersault on the way. 'It *must* be the superpower of agility again!'

But as he spoke, Finlay was picking up the huge boulder that Max had trodden on. He lifted it as though it was as light as a football and carried it in front of the gatehouse. 'No, it's not!' he exclaimed. 'It's strength!' He threw the boulder high up into the air and caught it easily on its way back down.

Max started to run over to him. The world blurred and in the blink of an eye he had jumped over the crack and was standing at Finlay's side.

'Wait a minute!' Finlay exclaimed. 'You just ran as quickly as I did when I had Hercules' superpower of speed, but we can't be super-strong and super-fast and super-agile . . .'

A thought burst into Max's brain. 'Unless the superpower we just took has somehow given us *all* Hercules' superpowers at the same time!' He shut his eyes to see if he was right. *Grow!* he thought, just as he had done the day he had had Hercules' size-shifting ability. A second later he was shooting upwards.

'Wicked!' Finlay gasped. 'We really *have* got all the powers. But how? Why?'

However, just then they heard a shout and looked behind them. Hercules had fallen on the ground. He had dropped his sword and shield. Juno was towering over him. Suddenly how and why didn't matter any more.

'Quick!' Max shouted. 'We've got to help Hercules!'

CHAPTER EIGHT

THE POWER OF FELLOWSHIP

Max and Finlay raced across the keep.
With their super-speed they reached the
tower in a split second. Finlay grabbed
Hercules' shield from the floor. *Shield me!*
he thought, just as Juno muttered, 'Freeze
him!' and clicked her fingers.

A magic barrier formed around
Finlay and Hercules. Juno's spell had no
effect.

She stared and backed off towards the gatehouse. 'No . . . that's impossible!'

Finlay felt like punching the air. He felt like he could do anything! Juno cast a fire bolt but it rebounded off the magic barrier. Letting the barrier down for a second, Finlay dodged across the keep, grabbed Hercules' sword and, in the blink of an eye, was back at the superhero's side.

'Here!' he gasped, pushing the sword and shield into Hercules' hands and helping Hercules to his feet.

'What has happened to you?' Hercules exclaimed. 'You seem to have superpowers of your own!'

'He's not the only one!' Max exclaimed, running over to the gatehouse and growing as tall as the tower.

'Superpowers or not, I will destroy

you!' Juno snarled. She raised her hands.

Grabbing an enormous armful of loose slabs from the roof of the gatehouse, Max tipped them on to Juno's head. They landed dead on target. With a startled cry,

the goddess collapsed under the weight of the stones. The fire bolt fell to the ground, burning a circle of grass away.

Max shrank to normal size and raced to where Finlay and Hercules were. 'Are you OK?' he demanded. He glanced nervously over his shoulder but Juno wasn't moving under all the rocks. He must have knocked her out!

'I am fine.' Hercules stared at him. 'But how do you both come to have these superpowers?'

The words burst out of Finlay. 'There was this new symbol on the gatehouse! It appeared after Juno's lightning bolt hit the wall.'

'We put our hands on it and suddenly found we could do all kinds of stuff,' added Max.

'What did the symbol look like?'
Hercules demanded.

'It was a picture of two hands around a
sword,' Finlay answered.

'The symbol of fellowship!' Hercules'
golden eyes widened with understanding.
'Without a superpower you had no
chance against Juno – it was not a fair
fight. The gods believe in fighting fair.
By placing the superpower there the
gods were giving you a chance in your
battle against her.'

Max frowned. 'How come we get to
have so many different powers all at once
although there was only one symbol?'

'Because it is the superpower of
fellowship,' Hercules replied. 'It is a very
fitting power for the gods to send. All
week you have shown true fellowship

– you have stood by each other, worked together, protected each other. This new superpower now allows you to fully share each other's experiences by both of you having all the superpowers that you have been using in the last seven days.'

CRASH!

They swung round at the sound of stones falling to the ground.

Juno was standing upright. She was covered with dust and her hair had come loose. It coiled around her shoulders like black snakes. Her eyes burnt with fury. 'It is time to finish this!' she shrieked. Shooting out her hand she let loose a fireball, straight at the two boys. They jumped apart and the fireball shot between them.

As they rolled over and leapt to their

feet she shot more bolts of burning fire at
them.

'Protect yourselves!' Hercules shouted.
'You do not need to be holding my
shield. You can both create barriers with
your minds!'

'I will kill you both!' Juno hissed as Max and Finlay dodged the balls of fire.

'You will never manage to kill them, Juno!' Hercules yelled. 'They are too strong for you.'

'What? These worms!' Juno exclaimed. 'Don't be ridiculous, Hercules!'

'They are brave and resourceful. They will outwit you!' Hercules declared. 'You will not succeed against them.'

Max frantically dodged a fireball. He wished Hercules would be quiet. The superhero just seemed to be making Juno even madder.

'You will never defeat them, Juno!' Hercules continued. 'Never!'

Max shook his head. What was Hercules doing?

Juno's face was consumed with

fury. 'We'll see about that!' she hissed.
Drawing herself up to her full height,
she opened her hands to reveal two
enormous bolts of burning white light.
She raised her arms and threw one at
each of the boys. 'Die, maggots!'

'No!' Max gasped, seeing the enormous
ball of fire hurtling towards Finlay.

'Max!' cried Finlay, staring in horror at
the lightning ball streaking towards his
friend.

'You know what to do, boys!' Hercules
roared.

'Shield!' they both shouted together.
And at exactly the same moment that
Max's hand shot out towards Finlay to
protect his friend, Finlay's hand shot out
towards him. Two silvery barriers formed
in front of each of them. The lightning

bolts banged into them and then shot
straight back towards Juno at twice the
speed and glowing twice as brightly. Juno
looked alarmed. She snapped her fingers.
A shield instantly formed in front of her
but the two bolts of bright light blasted
straight through it. They slammed into
the goddess, lifting her off her feet and

throwing her down to the crack in the ground.

'No!' she shrieked. The white light seemed to pin her to the ground. It streamed through her. Suddenly, there was a groaning, creaking noise and the crack widened. Juno screeched, but the next second she was falling into the hole below. Her twisted face vanished. The two sides of the crack swiftly moved back together, cutting off her enraged shriek. And then there was silence.

'She's gone,' Finlay breathed in shock.

Max stared at the ground. There was no crack. No trace of Juno. Only brown, withered grass.

CHAPTER NINE

SCARS

'W-what . . . what happened?' Max
stammered, swinging round to look at
Hercules.

There was a look of quiet satisfaction
on the superhero's face. 'Juno has been
defeated by her desire to destroy,' he
replied. 'Her own magic has imprisoned
her in the castle's underground
dungeon.'

'The dungeon!' Finlay exclaimed. 'We've been looking for that!'

'It is extremely well hidden under the ground. It has lain undisturbed for centuries,' said Hercules. 'And now that the crack has closed, hopefully it will stay that way.'

'But what actually happened?' Max insisted. 'How did the magic put her there?'

'Your powers collided,' answered Hercules. 'The superpower you have right now stems from goodness and loyalty. Juno's power stems from evil and selfishness. They are exact opposites; one cannot conquer the other, and they are equal in strength. But because you decided to protect each other, your power doubled and sent Juno's own destructive power back at her with

double the force. She could not defend
herself against it.'

'Did you know that would happen?'
Max asked, remembering how Hercules
had seemed to be goading Juno.

'I had an idea it might,' replied Hercules with a relieved smile. 'I knew that if she attacked you, your power would protect you. But I suspected somehow that you would protect each other and so make her own magic the cause of her downfall.' He smiled at them. 'In every task you have undertaken you have stood by each other with no thought to your own safety. You have acted with great loyalty.'

The boys looked at each other. 'We're friends,' Max said simply.

Finlay grinned at him. 'Yeah. Even if you do like patting mad bulls.'

'Least I don't try and climb trees with branches that are going to break!' Max grinned back. 'Or act like I think I'm a cowboy!'

'No, you just think you're a hotshot bullfighter!' Finlay teased.

'Cowboys?' Hercules said, looking confused. 'Bullfighters?'

'It's a long story,' Finlay grinned.

Hercules shook his head. 'I do not think I will ever fully understand you boys, but I know one thing for sure, you are both true heroes. I can never thank you enough for freeing me.'

'So what happens now?' Max asked.

'I must go back to making sure that the balance between good and evil is maintained in the world. I have won this fight against Juno, but the battle goes on as it has over the centuries. Still, for now, she must stay in the dungeon until she finds a way to break free.' Hercules looked at the tower. A smile played around his mouth. 'Or until she finds two willing helpers to help her get out!'

'Can't see that happening!' Max said. 'She'd deafen them with all her screeching!'

'What about the superpower?' Finlay asked hopefully. 'Can we keep it?'

But Hercules was shaking his head. 'I am afraid you must give it back to the gods. If you were to keep it you could not go back to your real life.'

Finlay was disappointed but not totally surprised. 'I guess it would be weird to have a superpower all the time,' he admitted, remembering how when he'd been super-fast it had made playing football at school very difficult because he couldn't run at normal speed.

'Place your hands on the gatehouse wall,' Hercules told them. 'On the same stone that you found the power.'

The boys looked at each other. 'Race you?' said Finlay.

'OK,' Max agreed eagerly.

A second later they were both standing in front of the gatehouse.

'Dead heat!' Max said.

For a moment, Finlay looked sad. 'I guess we're never going to be able to run that fast again.'

'No,' Max sighed. Having superpowers was amazing. He wished they could keep them forever but he knew Hercules was right. They couldn't. He looked at the gatehouse wall. 'Are you ready, Fin?'

Finlay nodded and together they placed

their hands on the stone they had taken
the superpower from. Warmth flooded
out of them into the wall. After a long
moment the stone turned cold under
their hands. They pulled their fingers
away. The shape of a sword clutched by

two hands glowed brightly and then the lines faded.

'It's gone,' Max said quietly.

'My skin still feels all weird though,' Finlay said slowly. 'Sort of tingly.'

'Mine too,' Max realized. 'But only bits of it.' He glanced down at his arm, which seemed to be prickling near the top, and stared. The wound that he had got while fighting a Man-Eating Bird two days ago was changing. The sore red edges were healing over and hardening and the wound was getting much smaller.

'Our wounds!' he exclaimed, looking at his leg and seeing that the wound that had been there had healed too. 'They're turning into scars.'

'Scars that are the same as the symbols of the superpowers we had,' Finlay

exclaimed, checking his own wounds.
'Look!' he pointed to his ankle, where
he now had a small scar in the shape
of a shield. He checked the wound
from the bull's horn – it was hardening
into a small scar in the shape of a
leaping stag.

'Your powers may have gone now,'
Hercules told them. 'But the scars
remain. They will stay with you forever,
badges of strength and honour,
reminding you of everything you
have learned and everything you have
achieved.'

'Wicked!' Finlay said in delight.

Max nodded. He had three real scars.
How cool was that? 'Guess they might be
tricky to explain when we get changed
for PE!' he said.

'They're quite small,' Finlay said thoughtfully. 'I bet no one will notice.'

'Until we show them!' Max added with a grin.

'I must leave you now. Thank you,' Hercules smiled at them and touched their shoulders briefly, 'my friends.'

Finlay smiled at him. 'See you around, Hercules!'

Hercules nodded gravely. 'Perhaps you shall. Farewell.' He clapped his hands and the next second he was gone.

The castle keep felt suddenly very empty. Max looked at Finlay. 'Wow! What a day!'

'What a week!' said Finlay.

'It's been fun, though,' said Max.

'If you like getting gored by bulls,' Finlay said.

'And savaged by sabre-toothed lions,' Max agreed.

'Not to mention being chased by giant pigs and Man-Eating Birds,' Finlay grinned.

Their eyes met. 'Maybe it'll be good to be normal again,' Max said.

Finlay nodded. His stomach rumbled. 'I'm starving.' He remembered something. 'Hey, we've still got our picnic to eat! There's all those sandwiches and cakes!'

'Yeah!' Max said. 'Let's go back and get the picnic hamper.'

'What did your mum put in the sandwiches, anyway?' Finlay asked.

'Roast beef,' Max replied.

'Lucky those bulls didn't notice or they might not have been too keen on following us!' Finlay chuckled.

Max looked at where the crack in
the ground had been. 'I guess we won't
be searching for the dungeon any
more.'

'No way,' Finlay said. 'Bye, Juno!'
He glanced at the grass. 'You're history.
Ancient history.'

'Only thing is, Fin,' Max said
thoughtfully, looking towards the
dungeon, 'my dad says that sometimes
history repeats itself.'

'I hope it doesn't this time,' said Finlay.
He stretched. 'Come on! I'm *starving*!
Last one to the picnic basket eats a fresh
cowpat!'

He raced towards the gatehouse. Max
sprinted after him.

Catching him up, he tried to push
him over. Finlay ducked and Max only

narrowly avoided skidding straight
through a pile of dung that one of the
bulls had left earlier. Shoving each other
and laughing, they crossed the bridge and
raced into the sunlight. Behind them a
furious shriek echoed around the castle's
empty keep.

ABOUT THE AUTHOR

ALEX CLIFF LIVES IN A VILLAGE IN
LEICESTERSHIRE, NEXT DOOR TO FIN AND
JUST DOWN THE ROAD FROM MAX, BUT
UNFORTUNATELY THERE IS NO CASTLE ON
THE OUTSKIRTS OF THE VILLAGE.
ALEX'S HOME IS FILLED WITH TWO
CHILDREN AND TWO LARGE AND VERY
SLOBBERY PET MONSTERS.

FIND OUT HOW THE ADVENTURE BEGAN, WHEN MAX AND FIN MET HERCULES AND FACED A ROARING LION IN ...

SUPER POWERS

ALEX CLIFF

DID YOU KNOW?

Hercules lived in Ancient Greece. He was the son of a woman named Alcmene and the god Zeus. When Hercules was a baby he could fight snakes with his bare hands! The labours he had to complete were originally set for him by his cousin Eurystheus, King of Mycenae.

THE BULLS OF GERYON

Hercules was told to steal the cattle belonging to the monster Geryon. To reach the island where the bulls were kept, Hercules had to travel from Greece to the tip of Spain where it meets Africa. From there he took a boat to Geryon's island, and faced many dangers – including Geryon himself – in order to herd the cattle back to Greece.

puffin.co.uk

YOUR
SUPER POWERS
QUEST

YOU NEED:

2 players
2 counters
1 dice
and nerves of steel!

YOU MUST:

Collect all **seven** superpowers
and save Hercules, who has
been trapped in the castle by
the evil goddess, Juno. All you
have to do is roll the dice and
follow the steps on the books
– try not to land on Juno's rock
or one of the monsters!

YOU CAN:

PLAY BOOK BY BOOK

The game is only complete when all seven books in the series are lined
up. But if you don't have them all yet, you can still complete the quests!
Whoever lands on the 'GO' rock first is the winner of that particular quest.

PLAY THE WHOLE GAME

Whoever collects all seven superpowers and is first to land on the final
rock has completed the entire quest and saved Hercules!

REMEMBER:

If you land on a 'Back to the Start' symbol, don't worry – you don't have
to go all the way back to book one – just back to the start of the game
on the book you are playing.

GOOD LUCK, SUPERHEROES!